MOUSE TIME

Rumer Godden is one of Britain's most distinguished authors, with many justly famous and much-loved books for both adults and children to her credit, including *The Diddakoi*, awarded the Whitbread Award for children's books in 1973, *Mr McFadden's Hallowe'en*, *A Kindle of Kittens*, *The Old Woman Who Lived in a Vinegar Bottle*, *Candy Floss & Impunity Jane*, *Listen to the Nightingale* and *Thursday's Children*.

Her two volumes of autobiography, *A Time to Dance, No Time to Weep* and *A House with Four Rooms* describe her long love affair with India and the years she spent as the director of the children's ballet school in Calcutta. They also show her affinity with animals, particularly Pekinese dogs, which she keeps as pets.

Rumer Godden now lives in Scotland, and is still writing new books for both adults and children.

MOUSE TIME

TWO STORIES BY

RUMER GODDEN

Illustrated by Jane Pinkney

MACMILLAN
CHILDREN'S BOOKS

Mouse Time was originally published in
two separate hardback volumes
by Macmillan & Co Ltd.
The Mousewife first published in Great Britain 1951
The Mousewife © 1951 Rumer Godden
Mouse House first published in Great Britain 1958
Mouse House © 1958 Rumer Godden

First published in hardback in 1993 by
Pan Macmillan Children's Books
This edition published 1995 by Macmillan Children's Books
a division of Macmillan Publishers Limited
25 Eccleston Place, London SW1W 9NF
and Basingstoke

Associated companies throughout the world

ISBN 0 330 7479 3

Illustrations copyright © 1993 Jane Pinkney

1 3 5 7 9 8 6 4 2

A CIP catalogue record for this book is available from
the British Library

Typeset by Intype, London
Printed and bound in Great Britain by
Cox & Wyman Ltd, Reading, Berkshire

CONTENTS

THE MOUSEWIFE

Wherever there is an old house with wooden floors and beams and rafters and wooden stairs and wainscots and skirting boards and larders, there are mice. They creep out on the carpets for crumbs, they whisk in and out of their holes, they run in the wainscot and between the ceiling and the floors. There are no signposts because they know the way, and no milestones because no one is there to see how they run.

In the old nursery rhyme, when the cat went to see the queen, he caught a little mouse under her chair; that was long, long ago and that queen was different from our queen, but the mouse was the same.

Mice have always been the same. There are no fashions in mice; they do not change. If a mouse could have a portrait painted of his great-great-grandfather, and *his* great-grandfather, it would be the portrait of a mouse today.

But once there was a little mousewife who was different from the rest.

She looked the same; she had the same ears and prick nose and whiskers and dewdrop eyes; the same little bones and grey fur; the same skinny paws and long skinny tail.

She did all the things a mousewife does: she made a nest for the mouse babies she hoped to have one day; she collected crumbs of food for her husband and herself; once she bit the tops off a whole bowl

of crocuses; and she played with the other mice at midnight on the attic floor.

'What more do you want?' asked her husband.

She did not know what it was she wanted, but she wanted more.

The house where these mice lived belonged to a spinster lady called Miss Barbara Wilkinson. The mice thought the house was the whole world. The garden and the wood that lay around it were as far away to them as the stars are to you, but the mouse-wife sometimes used to creep up on the windowsill and press her whiskers close against the pane.

In spring she saw snowdrops and apple blossoms in the garden and bluebells in the wood; in summer there were roses; in autumn all the trees changed colour; and in winter they were bare until the snow came and they were white with snow.

The mousewife saw all these through the window-pane, but she did not know what they were.

She was a house mouse, not a garden mouse or a field mouse; she could not go outside.

'I think about cheese,' said her husband. 'Why don't you think about cheese?'

Then, at Christmas, he had an attack of indigestion from eating rich crumbs of Christmas cake. 'There were currants in those crumbs,' said the mousewife.

'They have upset you. You must go to bed and be kept warm.' She decided to move the mousehole to a space behind the fender where it was warm. She lined the new hole with tufts of carpet wool and put her husband to bed wrapped in a pattern of grey flannel that Miss Wilkinson's lazy maid, Flora, had left in the dustpan. 'But I am grateful to Flora,' said the mousewife's husband as he settled himself comfortably in bed.

Now the mousewife had to find all the food for the family in addition to keeping the hole swept and clean.

She had no time for thinking.

While she was busy, a boy brought a dove to Miss

Wilkinson. He had caught it in the wood. It was a pretty thing, a turtledove. Miss Wilkinson put it in a cage on the ledge of her sitting-room window.

The cage was an elegant one; it had gilt bars and a door that opened if its catch was pressed down; there were small gilt trays for water and peas. Miss Wilkinson hung up a lump of sugar and a piece of fat. 'There, you have everything you want,' said Miss Barbara Wilkinson.

For a day or two the dove pecked at the bars and opened and shut its wings. Sometimes it called, 'Roo, coo, roo coo,' then it was silent.

'Why won't it eat?' asked Miss Barbara Wilkinson. 'Those are the very best peas.'

A mouse family seldom has enough to eat. It is difficult to come by crumbs, especially in such a neat, tidy house as Miss Barbara Wilkinson's. It was the peas that first attracted the attention of the mouse-wife to the cage when at last she had time to go up on the windowsill. 'I have been running here and there and everywhere to get us food,' she said, 'not allowing myself to come up on to the windowsill, and here are these fine peas, not to mention this piece of fat.' (She did not care for the sugar.)

She squeezed through the bars of the cage, but as she was taking the first pea from the tray, the dove moved its wings. I cannot tell you how quickly the mousewife pressed herself back through the bars and jumped down from the sill and ran across the floor and whisked into her hole. It was quicker than a cat can wink its eye. (She thought it was the cat.)

In spite of her great fright she could not help thinking of those peas. She was very hungry. 'I had better not go back,' she said. 'There is something dangerous there,' but back she went the very next day.

Soon the dove grew quite used to the mousewife's going in and out, and the mouse grew quite used to the dove.

'This is better,' said Miss Barbara Wilkinson. 'The dove is eating its peas,' but, of course, he was not; it was the mouse.

The dove kept his wings folded. The mousewife thought him large and strange and ugly with the speckles on his breast and his fine down. (She thought of it as fur, not feathers.) He was not at all like a mouse; his voice was deep and soft, quite unlike hers, which was a small, high squeaking. Most strange of all, to her, was that he let her take his peas; when she offered them to him he turned his head aside on his breast.

'Then at least take a little water,' begged the

mousewife, but he said he did not like water. 'Only dew, dew, dew,' he said.

'What is dew?' asked the mousewife.

He could not tell her what dew was, but he told her how it shines on the leaves and grass in the early morning for doves to drink. That made him think of night in the woods and of how he and his mate would come down with the first light to walk on the wet earth and peck for food, and of how, then, they would

17

fly over the fields to other woods farther away. He told this to the mousewife too.

'What is fly?' asked the ignorant little mousewife.

'Don't you know?' asked the dove in surprise. He stretched out his wings and they hit the cage bars. Still he struggled to spread them, but the bars were too close, and he sank back on his perch and sank his head on his breast.

The mousewife was strangely moved, but she did not know why.

Because he would not eat his peas, she brought him crumbs of bread and, once, a preserved blackberry that had fallen from a tart. (But he would not eat the blackberry.) Every day he talked to her about the world outside the window.

He told her of roofs and the tops of trees and of the rounded shapes of hills and the flat look of fields and of the mountains far away. 'But I have never flown as far as that,' he said, and he was quiet. He was thinking that now he never would.

To cheer him, the mousewife asked him to tell her about the wind; she heard it in the house on stormy nights, shaking the doors and windows with more noise than all the mice put together. The dove told her how it blew in the cornfields, making patterns in the corn, and of how it made different sounds in the

18

different sorts of trees, and of how it blew up the
clouds and sent them across the sky.

He told her these things as a dove would see them,
as it flew, and the mousewife, who was used to creep-
ing, felt her head growing as dizzy as if she were

spinning on her tail but all she said was, 'Tell me more.'

Each day the dove told her more. When she came he would lift his head and call to her, 'Roo coo, roo coo,' in his most gentle voice.

'Why do you spend so much time on the window-sill?' asked her husband. 'I do not like it. The proper place for a mousewife is in her hole or coming out for crumbs and frolic with me.'

The mousewife did not answer. She looked far away.

Then, on a happy day, she had a nestful of baby mice. They were not as big as half your thumb, and they were pink and hairless, with pink shut eyes and little pink tails like threads. The mousewife loved them very much. The eldest, who was a girl, she called Flannelette, after the pattern of grey flannel. For several days she thought of nothing and no one else. She was also busy with her husband. His digestion was no better.

One afternoon he went over to the opposite wall to see a friend. He was well enough to do that, he said, but certainly not well enough to go out and look for crumbs. The mice babies were asleep, the hole was quiet, and the mousewife began to think of the dove. Presently she tucked the nest up carefully and went up on the windowsill to see him; also she was hungry and needed some peas.

What a state he was in! He was drooping and nearly exhausted because he had eaten scarcely anything while she had been away. He cowered over her with his wings and kissed her with his beak; she had not known his feathers were so soft or that his breast was so warm. 'I thought you had gone, gone, gone,' he said over and over again.

'Tut! Tut!' said the mousewife. 'A body has other things to do. I can't be always running off to you,' but though she pretended to scold him, she had a tear at the end of her whisker for the poor dove. (Mouse tears look like millet seeds, which are the smallest seeds I know.)

She stayed a long time with the dove. When she went home, I am sorry to say, her husband bit her on the ear.

That night she lay awake thinking of the dove; mice stay up a great part of the night, but, toward dawn, they, too, curl into their beds and sleep. The mousewife could not sleep. She still thought of the dove. 'I cannot visit him as much as I could wish,' she said. 'There is my husband, and he has never bitten me before. There are the children, and it is surprising how quickly crumbs are eaten up. And no one would believe how dirty a hole can get if it is not attended to every day. But that is not the worst of it. The dove should not be in that cage. It is thoughtless of Miss Barbara Wilkinson.' She grew angry as she thought of it. 'Not to be able to scamper about the floor! Not to be able to run in and out, or climb up the larder to get at the cheese! Not to flick in and out and to whisk and to feel how you run in your tail! To sit in the trap until your little bones are stiff and your whiskers grow stupid because there is nothing for them to smell or hear or see!' The mousewife could only think of it as a mouse, but she could feel as the dove could feel.

Her husband and Flannelette and the other children were breathing and squeaking happily in their sleep, but the mousewife could hear her heart beating; the beats were little, like the tick of a watch, but they felt loud and disturbing to her. 'I cannot sleep,' said the mousewife, and then, suddenly, she felt she must go then, that minute, to the dove. 'It is too late. He will be asleep,' she said, but still she felt she should go.

She crept from her bed and out of the hole on to the floor by the fender. It was bright moonlight, so bright that it made her blink. It was bright as day, but a strange day, that made her head swim and her

tail tremble. Her whiskers quivered this way and that, but there was no one and nothing to be seen; no sound, no movement anywhere.

She crept across the pattern of the carpet, stopping here and there on a rose or a leaf or on the scroll of the border. At last she reached the wall and ran lightly up on to the windowsill and looked into the cage. In the moonlight she could see the dove sleeping in the feathers, which were ruffled up so that he looked plump and peaceful, but, as she watched, he dreamed and called 'roo coo' in his sleep and shivered as if he moved. 'He is dreaming of scampering and running free,' said the mousewife. 'Poor thing! Poor dove!'

She looked out into the garden. It too was as bright as day, but the same strange day. She could see the tops of the trees in the wood, and she knew, all at once, that was where the dove should be, in the trees and the garden and the wood.

He called 'roo coo' again in his sleep – and she saw that the window was open.

Her whiskers grew still and then they stiffened. She thought of the catch on the cage door. If the catch was pressed down, the door opened.

'I shall open it,' said the mousewife. 'I shall jump on it and hang from it and swing from it, and it will be pressed down; the door will open and the dove can come out. He can whisk quite out of sight. Miss Barbara Wilkinson will not be able to catch him.'

She jumped at the cage and caught the catch in her strong little teeth and swung. The door sprang open, waking the dove.

He was startled and lifted his wings, and they hit hard against the cage so that it shivered and the mousewife was almost shaken off.

'Hurry! Hurry!' she said through her teeth.

In a heavy sidelong way he sidled to the door and stood there looking. The mousewife would have given him a push, but she was holding down the catch.

At the door of the cage the dove stretched his neck toward the open window. 'Why does he not hurry?' thought the mousewife. 'I cannot stay here much longer. My teeth are cracking.'

He did not see her or look toward her; then – clap – he took her breath away so that she fell. He had opened his wings and flown straight out. For a moment he dipped as if he would fall, his wings were cramped, and then he moved them and lifted up and up and flew away across the tops of the trees.

The mousewife picked herself up and shook out her bones and her fur.

'So that is to fly,' she said. 'Now I know.' She stood looking out of the window where the dove had gone.

'He has flown,' she said. 'Now there is no one to tell me about the hills and the corn and the clouds. I shall forget them. How shall I remember when there is no one to tell me and there are so many

children and crumbs and bits of fluff to think of?'
She had millet tears, not on her whiskers but in her
eyes.

'Tut! tut!' said the mousewife and blinked them
away. She looked out again and saw the stars. It has

been given to few mice to see the stars; so rare is it that the mousewife had not even heard of them, and when she saw them shining she thought at first they must be new brass buttons. Then she saw they were very far off, farther than the garden or the wood, beyond the farthest trees. 'But not too far for me to see,' she said. She knew now that they were not buttons but something far and big and strange. 'But not so strange to me,' she said, 'for I have seen them. And I have seen them for myself,' said the mousewife, 'without the dove. I can see for myself,' said the mousewife, and slowly, proudly, she walked back to bed.

She was back in the hole before her husband woke up, and he did not know that she had been away.

Miss Barbara Wilkinson was astonished to find the cage empty next morning and the dove gone. 'Who could have let it out?' asked Miss Wilkinson. She suspected Flora and never knew that she was looking at someone too large and that it was a very small person indeed.

The mousewife is a very old lady mouse now. Her whiskers are grey and she cannot scamper any more; even her running is slow. But her great-great-grand-children, the children of the children of the children of Flannelette and Flannelette's brothers and sisters, treat her with the utmost respect.

She is a little different from them, though she looks the same. I think she knows something they do not.

This story is taken from one
written down in her journal
by Dorothy Wordsworth for
her brother William, the poet.
It was quite true, but her mouse,
I am sorry to say,
did not let the dove out of its cage.
I thought mine should, and she did.

R. G.

MOUSE HOUSE

Once upon a time there was a little mouse house. It was like a doll's house, but not for dolls, for mice.

Its walls were painted red, with lines for bricks. Its roof was grey, with painted tiles and a red chimney. The roof lifted up, and in the house was a hall with a front door, a sitting room, and a bedroom, each with a window.

The wallpaper had a pattern of spots as small as pinheads, and the carpets were pink flannel. In the hall was a doormat cut from two inches of tweed. The sitting room had a painted fireplace, two chairs, and a table. In the bedroom was a tiny looking glass and a bed with bedclothes and a blue and white quilt. At the window were muslin curtains, and on each sill stood thimble-sized pots of geraniums; the geraniums were made of scarlet silk. On tin-tack pegs on the wall hung some dusters no bigger than postage stamps.

Over the front door was a notice that said, 'MOUSE HOUSE'.

Mouse House was given to a girl called Mary as an Easter present. 'It's to keep your jewellery in,' said her father, but she shook her head.

'It's meant for mice,' said Mary, and indeed there were two mice there already, a he-mouse in the sitting room and a she-mouse in the bedroom. They wore clothes; He-mouse had a suit with a pale blue ribbon tie; She-mouse wore a dress with a pale blue apron. They stood on their hind legs, and their fur looked just like flannel, their whiskers looked like bristles, and their eyes were as still as beads.

'Are you proper mice?' asked Mary. There was no answer, not even a squeak.

He-mouse and She-mouse stayed quite still, quite, quite still.

Mary was disappointed. 'I thought mice ran,' she said.

Most mice do. They scamper up and down the stairs and come into the larder and the cupboards and climb the table legs. They whisk into holes and run behind the wainscoting. The sound of their running can make a rustle and patter like rain, and they go so fast you can hardly believe you have seen them. That is how most mice run, but not He-mouse and She-mouse.

Mary waited for them to move – 'Even a tail or a whisker,' said Mary. Sometimes she lifted the roof up quietly to take a sudden peep, but they were always standing where she had left them; still, quite, quite still.

At last she took Mouse House upstairs and put it away on her chest-of-drawers.

'Don't you want to play with it?' asked her mother.

'Mice can't play,' said Mary.

Far down, below-stairs, in Mary's house, was a

cellar where rubbish was kept, and there, behind an old broom in the corner, was another mouse house. It was not elegant like the one upstairs. It was a broken flowerpot made comfortable with hay. I cannot tell you how many mice lived in it because I was never quick enough to catch them, but it was brimful of mice.

'This overcrowding in houses is a terrible problem,' Mary's father said as he read the newspaper. The mice in the flowerpot could have told him that.

When they were all in it asleep there were always some whiskers or a tail hanging out, an ear, a paw, or a little mouse leg. There was not an eighth of an inch to spare – if you want to know how small that is, look on a school ruler – and the youngest, a little girl mouse called Bonnie, ended up most nights pushed out on the cellar floor.

'She will catch cold,' said Mother Mouse. 'It's bad to lie out on the stone.'

Father Mouse scolded the children. 'Naughty! Bad mice!' he said.

'They can't help it,' said Mother Mouse. 'There are too many of them.'

Then he scolded her. 'You shouldn't have had so many,' he said.

But they were beautiful children. Their fur was soft and brown, not at all like flannel; their ears and tails were apple-blossom pink; and their whiskers were fine, not like bristles. Their eyes were black and busy, not still, like beads, and all day those mouse children darted and scampered and played. Mary would not have believed her eyes if she had seen them. Even when they were asleep they scrabbled and twitched as if they were running in their dreams. 'But I wish they wouldn't,' said Bonnie.

'Couldn't we move to a larger house?' she asked. 'Couldn't we find one? Couldn't we *look*?' asked Bonnie. But there was no time; with such a big family to feed, Father and Mother Mouse were gathering crumbs and bits of cheese and scraps of this and that from morning to night.

'A-t-*choo*!' sneezed Bonnie.

What games did the mice children play? Much the same as you: catch-as-catch-can and puss-in-the-corner – though puss was really frightening to them. They played I'm-on-Tom-Cat's-Ground-Picking-up-Gold-and-Silver, and blind-mouse-buff and hide-and-seek. Mary would have been surprised. An empty matchbox made them a cart, and for balls they had some dried peas.

'Come and play, Bonnie!' cried her brothers and sisters, but Bonnie had caught a cold and did not want to play. Two tears as small as dew-drops ran down her whiskers; mice do not have handkerchiefs, so that she could not wipe them away.

That night she found herself out on the floor again. 'Mammy! Mammy!' squeaked Bonnie, but Mother Mouse was asleep, worn out with searching for crumbs and cheese.

'Mammy! Mammy!'

The cellar was cold and dark. From inside the flowerpot came soft snufflings and squealings, the sound of little mice happily asleep. Bonnie tried to get back, but she could not push in more than the tip of her nose.

'Where can I go?' squeaked Bonnie.

She wrapped herself round in her tail and curled up on the cellar floor, but it was too cold to sleep. She tried once more to push back into the flowerpot, but one of her brothers, dreaming of the cat, kicked her

hard in the eye with his paw. 'Ouch!' squeaked
Bonnie, but no mouse heard.

'Nobody wants me,' said poor Bonnie and began
to creep away. 'Where can I go?' she asked; there
was no mouse to tell her.

She crept across the cellar floor until she came to
a flight of steps. 'Shall I go up them?' asked Bonnie.
There seemed nowhere else to go.

At the top she rubbed her whiskers; she thought a strange light was shining. 'Is it?' asked Bonnie, straining her whiskers to look.

The light was shining at the end of a long passage; it came from under the crack of a door.

A mouse can wriggle under a crack. Bonnie crept down the passage and under the crack and found herself in the hall.

The hall was filled with clear silver light. Bonnie blinked. She had not seen moonlight before. It was very pretty but very strange. It turned her into a silver mouse, and that made her feel dizzy.

She crept out on the rug. She had never been here before – only behind the wainscot – and her whiskers trembled as she looked this way and that.

The grandfather clock in the corner went TOCK-TOCK-TOCK-TOCK, and Bonnie's heart, which was not much bigger than a watch, went *tick-tick-tick-tick-tick-tick*, far more quickly. Then it almost stopped.

The cat was asleep on a chair.

Bonnie had only heard about the cat; she had never seen him; but she knew at once what he was.

W-H-I-S-K! I wish I could describe to you how quickly she was gone up the stairs.

Oh, how her legs ached and her breath hurt! It was like climbing a mountain far too fast.

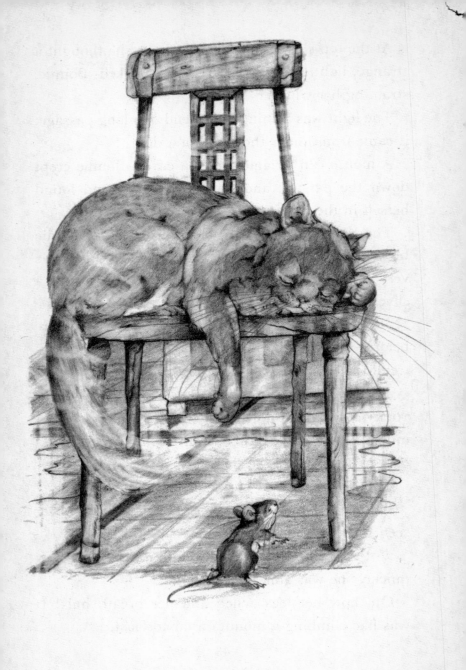

'He's coming! He's coming!' squeaked Bonnie.

The cat had not moved an eyelid, but Bonnie was half dead with fright when she reached the top landing. 'A hole! I need a hole!' she squeaked, but there was no time to look for one, and she wriggled under the crack of the nearest door – it was the door of Mary's room.

'I need somewhere high and safe. Another mountain!' And Bonnie ran up the highest thing she could see – it was the chest-of-drawers.

'Oh, my poor heart!' cried Bonnie; it was going *tick-tick-tick-tick-tick*, *tick-tick-tick-tick-tick* faster than you can say it. Then, there in front of her, she saw Mouse House.

'It's a hole! It's a house!' cried Bonnie.

The front door was open, and she flicked inside.

For a long time she lay in the hall. Then, when she was sure she was really safe, she sniffed the doormat with her whiskers.

She looked into the sitting room. He-mouse was there.

'Hello,' said Bonnie.

There was no answer.

She touched He-mouse with her whiskers – which

45

is the mouse way of shaking hands – but he did not touch her back.

'It looks like a mouse, but it does not feel like a mouse nor smell like a mouse,' said Bonnie.

She went into the bedroom. She-mouse was there.

'Hello,' said Bonnie.

There was no answer.

Bonnie touched She-mouse with her whiskers, but She-mouse did not touch her back.

'It looks like a mouse, but it does not feel like a mouse nor smell like a mouse,' said Bonnie.

'Can't you hear me?' Bonnie asked.

She-mouse did not say 'Yes,' and she did not say 'No'; she said nothing at all.

'Pay attention,' said Bonnie and flipped She-mouse with her tail.

She-mouse fell flat on her back on the floor.

Bonnie went back into the sitting room, where He-mouse had not moved.

'You had better lie down too,' said Bonnie and flipped *him* with her tail.

He-mouse fell flat on his back on the floor.

That made Bonnie remember how much she wanted to lie down herself, not stiff and straight as they did, but curled up soft and warm. 'Aaaahh!' She gave a yawn.

She tried to lie on the chairs, but they were too small. The table was too hard. She went into the bedroom and looked at herself in the glass, and the mouse in the glass gave a yawn too. 'Poor little mouse. How sleepy you are!' said Bonnie. Then she turned and saw the bed.

She had not seen a bed before, but she knew at once what it was for. Whisk! Up she jumped and wriggled under the quilt. It is true that she put her tail on the pillow, but a very young mouse cannot be expected to know everything.

The bed was soft, the quilt was warm; in a minute Bonnie was fast asleep.

She was so tired, that she slept a long, long time. When she woke up in the morning, someone had shut the front door.

Have you ever been shut in? Then you will know how it feels. Bonnie ran around from room to room, round and round and round. She pressed her face against the windows until her whiskers hurt; she bruised her paws in beating on the door.

The table and chairs, the bed and the geraniums were all knocked over; the looking glass came off the wall and the dusters were twitched off their pegs. The wallpaper was scratched off and the carpets were torn.

'Let me out! Let me out!' squeaked Bonnie, but nobody heard. There was no one to hear. Mary had gone down to breakfast.

He-mouse and She-mouse lay flat on the floor; Bonnie ran over and over them, but they did not protest.

'Mammy! Mammy!' squeaked Bonnie. 'I want to go home.'

Far down below in the cellar Mother Mouse was squeaking.

'Be quiet and let me sleep,' said Father Mouse, but she would not let him sleep.

'A mouse child is missing,' she squeaked, and she shook him. 'A mouse child is missing, is missing!'

'How do you know?' asked Father Mouse, and he tumbled slowly out of bed. He slept in the bottom of the flowerpot and got up last of all.

'I counted them,' said Mother Mouse.

'*You* can't count,' said Father Mouse. Neither could he, but he did not tell her that. He watched the mice children hopping and skipping about. 'They are all here,' he said.

But Mother Mouse shook her whiskers. 'There should be one more.' She pulled all the hay out of the flowerpot; there were some bits of cheese rind, but no mouse child was there. She wept, but Father Mouse quickly ate up the cheese rind. It was his private store.

*

Upstairs in Mouse House Bonnie ran round and round.

When the flowerpot was empty, how dirty and small it looked. 'How can anyone be expected to bring up children in *that*?' said Mother Mouse.

'What's the matter with it?' asked Father.

'It's dirty and shabby and broken and small,' said Mother Mouse. 'There's a hole in the bottom – a little mouse could fall straight through it or be cut on the jagged edges or fall out on the cellar floor. You must find me another house at once!' said Mother Mouse.

'What *me*?' asked Father Mouse. 'I'm eating.' And I am sorry to say that with his mouth full he said, 'The houth ith for the children. Leth the children look.'

The mouse children were delighted. 'A new house? We'll find one!' they cried and ran squeaking all over the cellar floor.

They found an old coal scuttle, but it was full of soot. 'We should be black mice,' said Mother Mouse.

They found a flour bin with a hole in it, but all the flour had not run out. 'We should be white mice,' said Mother Mouse.

A riding boot looked cosy, but: 'What a long long

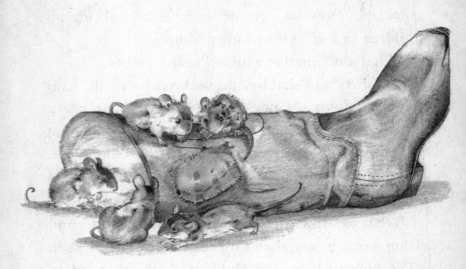

passage,' said Mother Mouse. 'And it's dark. It needs a window at the other end.'

There was no more room in a kettle than in the flowerpot, and a dustpan was not the right shape.

'It's too difficult to find a house,' said the mouse children. They lay down in the hay and went to sleep. Father Mouse slept too, but Mother Mouse sat up. She wanted a new house and she was missing her baby. Every now and again a mouse tear slid to the end of her whiskers.

And upstairs in Mouse House poor Bonnie ran round and round. 'Let me out! Let me out!' she squeaked.

Every morning after breakfast Mary made her bed. This morning, when she came into the room, she heard a queer noise; it was rustlings and scratchings and thumps and squeaks. It seemed to come from Mouse House. Mary listened: squeaks and thumps and scratchings and rustlings, and it did come from Mouse House! 'My mice are *playing*!' cried Mary.

She ran to lift up the roof and look . . . and nearly dropped it.

Quick as a flash, with a flip and a thud, Bonnie had jumped out. WHISK! She ran down the chest-of-drawers and out through the bedroom door. All Mary saw was a flash of whisker and tail.

'They've gone!' cried Mary, but when she turned over the mess in Mouse House, He-mouse and She-mouse were flat on the floor.

'Then was there *another* mouse? asked Mary.

What a sight Mouse House was now! The curtains were down, the paper was in ribbons, and the carpets were ripped. Chairs and bedclothes, geraniums and dusters were all mixed up; the legs had come off the table; the quilt was torn to bits. 'It's all spoiled,' said Mary.

There was nothing to do with Mouse House but to put it down in the cellar.

Bonnie took a long time to reach home. She ran into a hole in the wainscot on the landing and lost her way. All day she trotted up and down those wainscot passages. Once she came out into the hall and met the cat; then she got into the bathroom where a lady was washing in the basin 'A mouse! A mouse!' screamed the lady and threw a sponge. The sponge landed on the floor by Bonnie and made her soaking wet.

It was not until late that evening that a tired, cold, dirty, draggled little mouse put her whiskers out of another hole and found she was in the cellar. She was just going to run to the flowerpot, when what did she see?

She shook her whiskers once, twice, three times before she could believe her eyes. The flowerpot was gone, and where it had stood, under the old broom, was Mouse House.

But what a different Mouse House! It was full of scufflings and squeakings; out of every window and even up the chimney peeped little mice. Father Mouse was in the hall, and on the doorstep Mother Mouse was looking anxiously this way and that.

'Mammy! Mammy!' squeaked Bonnie.

'I *knew* there was one more!' said Mother Mouse.

For the mice, Mouse House was not spoiled at all; they found it far more convenient without curtains and a table and chairs.

They used one room for sleeping in, the other as a pantry. 'That's better,' said Mother Mouse. 'It *is* better not to have cheese rind in the beds.' Father Mouse hid a little under the doormat in the hall.

The scraps of wallpaper and carpet and bedclothes made a comfortable nest; the girl mice wrapped each of the geraniums in a duster and used them for dolls.

What happened to He-mouse and She-mouse? Mary had lifted them out of the house at once but they did not seem to notice when it was taken away, or that He-mouse's tie was off and She-mouse's apron torn. 'And it wasn't *you* playing,' said Mary.

She tidied them up and sewed them on a pin-cushion and gave it to her aunt for Christmas.

The mice are very happy, particularly Bonnie. She was a little nervous at first of being shut into Mouse House, but the door soon came off its hinges, with the mouse traffic going in and out. When her brothers and sisters heard the story they voted she should sleep in the bed. 'So that she can never be pushed out again,' said Mother Mouse.

'But if I hadn't been pushed out,' said wise little Bonnie, 'we shouldn't have Mouse House.'

How do I know all this? Well, one day, not a long time after, Mary hid in the cellar when *she* played hide-and-seek. As she sat there, quite quiet, the mice children came hopping out; hopping and skipping and scampering and jumping. 'Then mice *do* play,' said Mary.

After that she would often steal down to watch and listen and look.

'They are *my* mice,' said Mary. 'I gave them Mouse House.'

Then she stopped and thought, Or did one little mouse come and fetch it?

When she had thought that, I think she could guess the rest, and that is how she came to tell me, and I to tell you, the story of Mouse House.

Rumer Godden
Candy Floss and Impunity Jane

If you were a doll would you like to ride on a horse and live at the fair – or be
taken home by Clementina, a rich little girl?

And, imagine, if you were a doll would you prefer to sit on a bead cushion for
over fifty years – or go on adventures with a boy called Gideon?

Two china dolls, Candy Floss and Impunity Jane, know what *they* would like
best. And dolls' wishes can be very strong indeed . . .

Dyan Sheldon
Lilah's Monster

Lilah was a perfect little girl. She was never dirty, noisy or rude. She was *always* neat. Lilah kept her shoes in a row on her shoe rack, and her books in a row on her shelf. Her games were in a box marked 'toys'. And her monster was kept in the back of the cupboard.

Lilah's monster's name was Annabel. Annabel was a perfect monster . . .

Maggie Pearson
The Puddletown Dragon

The dragons are flying north for the spring, led by Great-grandmother
Scorcher. Suddenly, Smallest-of-all runs out of puff and falls from the sky —
right on top of Puddletown.

Nobody notices him until they see his shadow which is HUGE!

First there is PANIC . . . Then Puddletown becomes famous. And *everyone* is
hunting for the dragon.

Everyone except Alice. She *knows* where he is. But the adults won't listen to
her . . .